CAKE

For Chris Inns and Laura Roberts—
thank you for helping us to bake our little cake

ALADDIN
An imprint of Simon & Schuster Children's Publishing Division
1230 Avenue of the Americas, New York, New York 10020
This Aladdin hardcover edition March 2019
Copyright © 2018 by Sue Hendra and Paul Linnet
Originally published in Great Britain in 2018 by Macmillan Children's Books
All rights reserved, including the right of reproduction in whole or in part in any form.
ALADDIN and related logo are registered trademarks of Simon & Schuster, Inc.
For information about special discounts for bulk purchases, please contact
Simon & Schuster Special Sales at 1-866-506-1949 or business@simonandschuster.com.
The Simon & Schuster Speakers Bureau can bring authors to your live event.
For more information or to book an event contact the Simon & Schuster Speakers Bureau
at 1-866-248-3049 or visit our website at www.simonspeakers.com.
The text of this book was set in Meltura.
Manufactured in China 0119 MCM
2 4 6 8 10 9 7 5 3 1
This book has been cataloged with the Library of Congress.
ISBN 978-1-5344-2550-7 (hc)
ISBN 978-1-5344-2551-4 (eBook)

Sue Hendra & Paul Linnet
CAKE

Aladdin
New York   London   Toronto   Sydney   New Delhi

Cake had just received an exciting invitation.

He'd never been to a party before,
so he didn't know what to expect.
But he was sure about one thing—
he wanted to look his best.

Fish didn't know what Cake should wear.
He'd never been to a party either.

"Hmmm . . . ," said Fish.

"Nope."

"I don't think so."

"What about a hat?" suggested Fish.

"Good thinking!" said Cake.

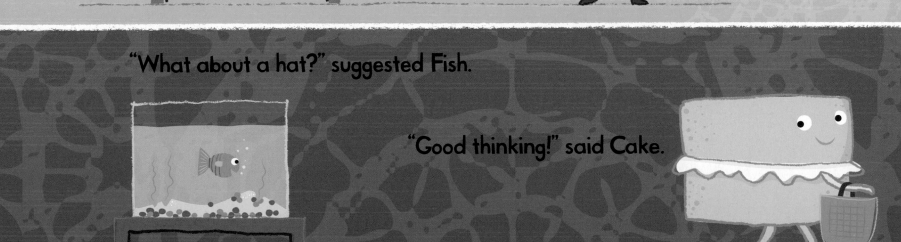

So off Cake went to buy a hat.

Cake tried on lots of hats in the shop.

But none of them were quite right.

"Is it for a special occasion?" asked the shop assistant. "A wedding, perhaps?"

"No," said Cake, "a party."

"Oh," said the shop assistant. "In that case, I have just the thing."

And he disappeared out the back.

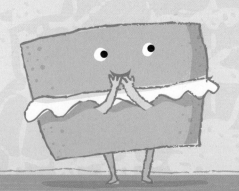

"Here you go, sir," said the shop assistant.
"You'll be irresistible in this."

"Thank you very much,"
said Cake.

He couldn't wait to
get home and show
Fish his new hat.

"Are you ready?" Cake called from his bathroom.

"TA-DA!"

"You've done it!" shouted Fish.

Cake was soon on his way to the party,
dressed in his new hat.

"Deedly-dee, deedly-dum, I'm off to a party to have some fun!"

Cake was a bit nervous
when he arrived.

But when everyone saw him, they cheered!
"CAKE'S HERE! A party isn't a party without
CAKE!" they said. And in he went.

Cake was having so much
fun at the party.

There was dancing,

and lots of games.

But then the singing started. . . .

"Happy birthday to you,

happy birthday to you . . . "

Cake was getting a bad feeling about this.

"Oh, crumbs!"

Suddenly there was a gust of wind and everything went . . .

BLACK!

Then there was a smell of raspberries . . .

and Cake felt a wibbly-wobbly
hand grab hold of his,

and a wibbly-wobbly
voice said . . .

"QUICK!

Run for it, Cake!"